SUPERMAN

LAST SON OF kRYPTON

WRITTEN BY
MICHAEL DAHL

ILLUSTRATED BY
JOHN DELANEY AND
LEE LOUGHRIDGE

SUPERMAN CREATED BY
JERRY SIEGEL AND
JOE SHUSTER

STONE ARCH BOOKS
MINNEAPOLIS   SAN DIEGO

Published by Stone Arch Books in 2009
151 Good Counsel Drive, P.O. Box 669
Mankato, Minnesota 56002
www.stonearchbooks.com

Library of Congress Cataloging-in-Publication Data
Dahl, Michael.
    Last Son of Krypton / by Michael Dahl; illustrated by John Delaney.
    p. cm. — (DC Super Heroes. Superman)
    ISBN 978-1-4342-1155-2 (library binding)
    ISBN 978-1-4342-1370-9 (pbk.)
    [1. Superheroes—Fiction.] I. Delaney, John, ill. II. Title.
PZ7.D15134Las 2009
[Fic]—dc22   2008032418

Summary: The distant planet Krypton faces total destruction. Before it
explodes, the scientist Jor-El and his wife Lara send their only son into
outer space. Later, the child's rocket crashes into a Kansas cornfield where
a farmer and his wife discover the boy and his strange powers.

Art Director: Bob Lentz
Designer: Bob Lentz

1 2 3 4 5 6 14 13 12 11 10 09

Printed in the United States of America

TABLE OF CONTENTS

CHAPTER 1

THE DYING PLANET

"Our world is doomed!" said Jor-El. He faced a group of leaders and scientists on his home planet of Krypton. He spoke with anger, not in fear.

"The fate of this planet, and everyone on it, rests in your hands," Jor-El continued. "Earthquakes have rocked Krypton for many months. Tidal waves have flooded our coastlines. Volcanoes have erupted at the edges of our cities. If we do not act now, everything we have worked for will be destroyed!"

Behind the group of scientists stood a strange, metal figure. The figure, a supercomputer in the shape of a man, stepped forward. His metal head and glowing eyes towered above Jor-El.

"This is nonsense, Jor-El," said the supercomputer. "Krypton has revolved around her red sun for millions of years. Our planet will continue to revolve for a million more. Safely and peacefully."

"Not according to my research," said Jor-El.

"Your research is wrong," said Brainiac calmly. "My brain has been going over your figures for the past several weeks. And the answer I come up with is this: Krypton is simply going through a phase. In a few months, the volcanic activity will stop."

"That's impossible," said Jor-El.

Brainiac's eyes glowed brightly. "Have I ever been wrong before?" he asked.

Jor-El was silent.

"I am not wrong this time, either," said Brainiac.

As the metal man spoke, the crowd nodded. They were calmed by his words.

"With all due respect, there is always a first time for being wrong," warned Jor-El. "The pressure inside our planet is growing. This is *not* simply a phase. This is the entire destruction of our world. We must leave Krypton before it explodes!"

Someone in the chamber cried out in alarm. A murmur of panic passed through the crowd. Brainiac raised his hands.

"Jor-El fills you with fear," Brainiac said. "He controls you by frightening you."

"No!" said Jor-El. "I do not seek power. I only seek the safety of my fellow citizens."

"If you care for their safety, then you will keep silent," said Brainiac. The lights in his metal skull were blinking angrily.

Another figure stood up. It was Vond-a, leader of the science council. She stepped onto the floor and stood between Jor-El and the robot.

"I agree with Brainiac," she said. "Your words will only panic the good people of Krypton, Jor-El. If Brainiac's supercomputer brain tells him that the planet is safe, then it is safe."

Jor-El knew it was useless to argue. He had been warning the scientists for weeks.

The scientists never listened. Now, Jor-El bowed his head. He said, "I will obey the decision of the council." Quietly, he left the chamber.

Brainiac watched Jor-El walk away. Dark thoughts hummed through the supercomputer's brain. *Jor-El is right,* he thought to himself. *Krypton will explode. But these fools must never know.* An evil smile crossed Brainiac's face. *Jor-El must be silenced.*

CHAPTER 2

A SPACESHIP TOO SMALL

Miles away, Jor-El stepped out of his flyer pod. He entered his living chambers. His wife, Lara, greeted him nervously.

"Did the council listen to you, Jor-El?" she asked.

Jor-El shook his head. "They listened to Brainiac instead," he said. "He doesn't understand the danger we're in. Something must be wrong with his programming."

Suddenly, the house shook. Several windows on the floor above them shattered.

"Another earthquake," said Lara.

The shaking stopped as quickly as it began. "I've been tracking quakes all over Krypton," she added. "They're growing stronger. There are more of them. Your calculations are right, Jor-El."

The couple hurried to their lab. "There's no comfort in being right," Jor-El said. "Especially when it means our world will be destroyed."

Jor-El checked his monitors. "I'm afraid it's worse than I thought, Lara," he said. "Krypton's core is heating up. The pressure is growing faster than I predicted."

"What does that mean?" Lara asked.

"Krypton will explode in a matter of days, possibly even hours," he said.

"What about our son?" Lara gasped.

Jor-El nodded. "We must get him at once and bring him to the launch port," he said.

Lara rushed down the stairs to the nursery. Before she entered the room, she smiled. She could hear their infant son cooing happily in his crib.

"Kal-El," she called.

The baby boy turned at the sound of his mother's voice. A wide grin stretched across his face. He held out his arms, wanting to be picked up.

"Oh, Kal-El," whispered Lara. She held the child tightly to her chest. "What a good boy you are."

Lara quickly grabbed some red and blue blankets to wrap the baby in. Then she hurried to the launch port to join her husband.

The port was at the top of their living quarters. A wide, open window showed a view of the entire city.

Lara entered the port. She saw Jor-El working on the model of a transport rocket ship. She hugged the baby even tighter.

"I had hoped that we would have time to build larger transports," said Jor-El. "They could have safely carried our people to another planet. To a new home."

"Now," he added, "this small model can carry only one." Jor-El looked down at his smiling son. The baby wrapped a tiny hand around his father's finger.

Another quake rocked the building. A light fell from the ceiling and crashed at Lara's feet. The baby cried out. "Jor-El, we must hurry," Lara said.

Jor-El checked the control panel for the rocket launcher. Lara placed the baby's blankets inside the ship. She made a warm, inviting nest to hold her son. Then she stared at the boy as he sat on a nearby table. "You have no idea how important you are, do you?" she said. "Kal-El, you are Krypton's last hope."

Another crash echoed throughout the building. Lara quickly scooped up her son.

"That wasn't an earthquake," said Jor-El.

"It came from downstairs," said Lara.

Jor-El switched on a video monitor. The monitor was connected to a camera built into their front door. As soon as the monitor blinked on, Lara grabbed her husband's arm.

Vond-a, the head of the science council, stood outside their living quarters. Standing with her was a squad of security troopers, fully armed.

"Jor-El!" she shouted. "Open the door! Your family is under arrest!"

CHAPTER 3

ESCAPE!

Outside Jor-El's and Lara's living quarters, the troopers were startled by a new noise.

zWWWwOOOOMMMM!

A fiery object flew across the sky.

"Is that a meteor?" asked one of the troopers.

"No meteors were predicted at this time," replied Vond-a. Just then, another tremor rocked the planet. The troopers were thrown off their feet.

Miles above them, the flaming object flew out of Krypton's atmosphere. The council leader was correct. It was not a meteor. It was a spaceship. And inside the ship was the supercomputer Brainiac.

It would be a shame if I stayed behind and was destroyed, thought Brainiac. *My super brain is worth more than a million of those puny humans.*

He set his ship's controls to take him to a distant galaxy called the Milky Way. "The advanced knowledge of Krypton shall survive in me. With that knowledge, I will conquer another world," he thought.

Brainiac's ship streaked through Krypton's sky. Meanwhile, Jor-El checked the controls of the smaller ship in his launch port.

"It's almost ready," he said to Lara.

His wife was saying good-bye to their infant son. The baby lay inside the ship. He was wrapped in a cocoon of red and blue blankets.

"Be good, Kal-El," she said. Her eyes filled with tears. "You will find a new home, a safe place far away from here."

A loud crash sounded below. The security troopers had knocked down the front door.

Jor-El pressed a remote control. The doors of the small ship closed with a hissing sound. The lock clicked. Then a loud humming filled the room.

As the humming grew louder, the ship lifted into the air. Little Kal-El was unaware of what was happening to him.

Kal-El rested in his soft blankets. He was secure inside the unbreakable walls of his father's creation.

"Don't be afraid," Jor-El said, turning to his wife. "We will always be a part of Kal-El."

Lara gazed at the rising ship. "We will never forget you, my son," she said.

"There they are!" A trooper was standing at the door of the port.

He pointed into the room at Jor-El and Lara. The rest of the squad gathered behind him. They drew weapons and marched into the room.

"Move away from the controls, Jor-El!" commanded Vond-a.

"Don't, Jor-El!" shouted Lara.

"Stay out of this, Lara," said Vond-a. "Your husband is a danger to the planet of Krypton."

"You are the danger to Krypton!" cried Lara. "My husband was only trying to save us. And now he is trying to save —"

"Quiet, Lara," said her husband.

The council leader looked around at Jor-El's scientific equipment. "What is going on here?" she asked. "And what is that ship doing?" She pointed at the object floating high above the floor.

The troopers aimed their blasters at the small craft. "It is obviously some kind of weapon," said Vond-a. "Shoot it down."

"No!" Lara screamed. Jor-El threw himself in front of the troopers.

A bright light filled the room.

The small ship flashed out of the room. It flew with such force that everyone inside the launch room was hurled against the walls. Outside, the ship streaked through the sky. It looked like a shooting star.

Faster and faster, the ship raced above the surface of the planet. It rose above the vast cities. It rushed past the highest clouds. Within seconds, it was speeding past Krypton's three moons.

Gazing into the sky, Jor-El and Lara followed the trail of their vanishing son. They held onto each other. A powerful quake shook the city. The walls were torn away from their building. The rays of the planet's red sun filled the launch room, turning it the color of blood.

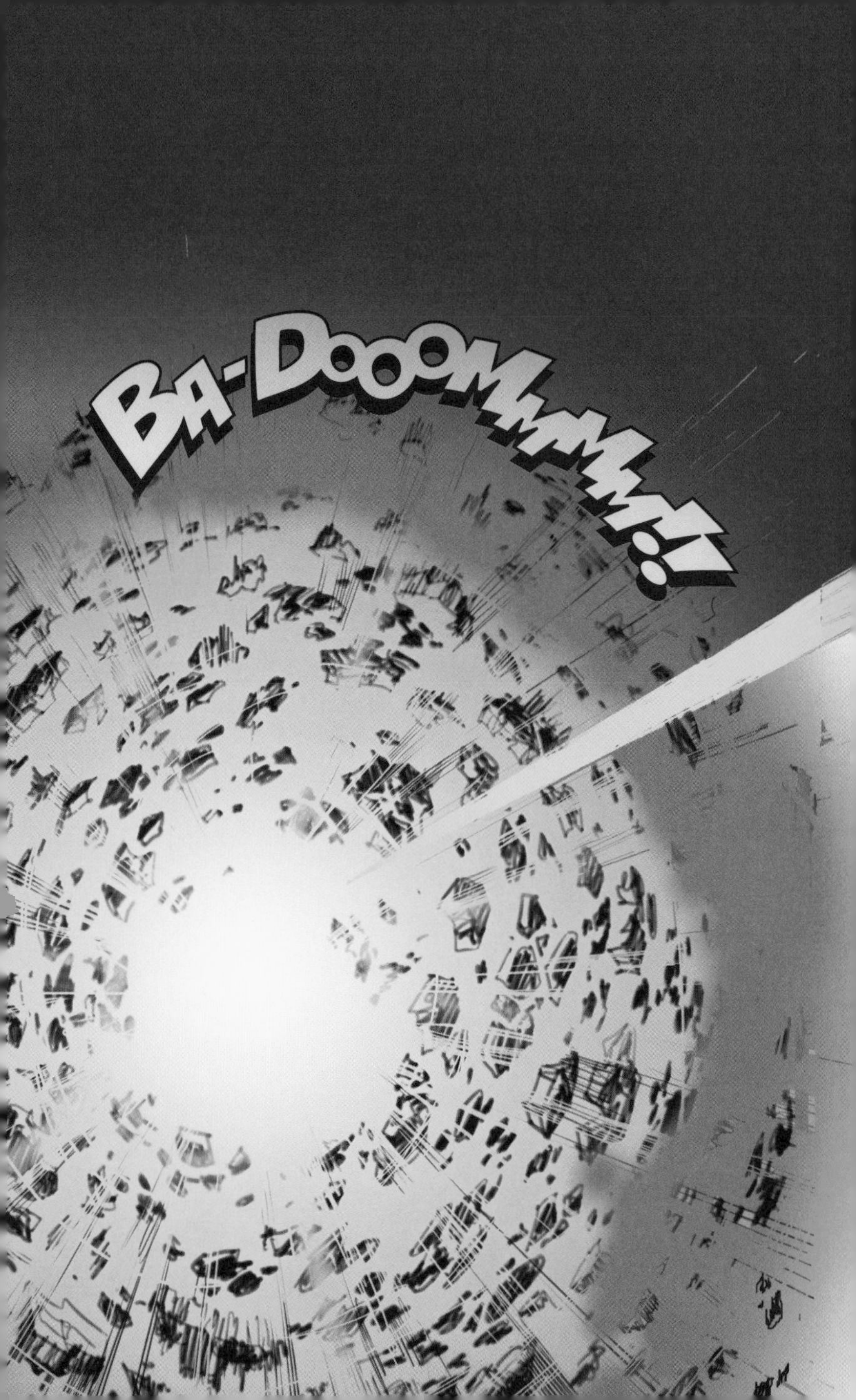
BA-DOOOMMMM!!

"Good-bye, Kal-El," Jor-El whispered.

As Krypton's greatest scientist had predicted, the huge planet exploded. Continents were ripped apart by volcanic force. The oceans evaporated. The sky itself caught on fire. A billion lives were lost in a second. But one small life sailed swiftly away to another planet.

CHAPTER 4

A NEW HOME

It was a summer day in Kansas. A yellow sun floated in the blue, hazy sky. The hot sun beat down on the fields around the town of Smallville.

On a farm outside of town, Jonathan Kent stared at the rows and rows of corn. He was sitting in the cab of his combine. He had been driving up and down the rows of corn for hours.

He had farmed these fields for many years. He wondered how many more years he would be driving this combine.

BZZZT! His cell phone rang. Jonathan pulled it from his belt. "What is it, Martha?" he said.

"How did you know it was me?" asked his wife on the other end.

"Who else would it be?" Jonathan said with a smile. "You're the only one who ever calls me on this thing."

"You could at least be polite and say hello," said Martha Kent.

 THWOOOOMMM!!

"What was that?" yelled Jonathan.

A fiery ball rushed past the cab of the combine. It missed hitting Jonathan by just a few feet.

"Jonathan, are you all right?" yelled Martha's voice from the phone.

"I don't know," he said. "I think I just saw a meteor."

"It's a meteor all right," said Martha. "I can see it from the kitchen window."

The combine was thrown into the air. Jonathan braced himself against the cab's door. Martha screamed. Cows in a nearby meadow tipped over. From the edge of the field, smoke and flames could be seen.

"Whatever it was," Jonathan said to himself, "I think it just landed."

A few minutes later, Martha joined her husband in the field. They walked carefully toward the rising smoke. The meteor had dug a huge crater in the soil.

When they came near the edge of the crater, the Kents stopped.

"Maybe we should call the police," said Martha. "Or a science teacher from the junior college."

"I don't believe it," said Jonathan.

He took off his glasses and wiped them with a rag. "That doesn't look like a meteor to me," Jonathan added.

"What's it supposed to look like?" asked Martha.

"A rock, Martha. A big ugly rock. But this is smooth and shiny." Jonathan took a step forward. "Oww," he groaned.

"Careful," said his wife. "You got banged up in that combine."

"I'll be careful," he said.

The object was smooth and shiny, as Jonathan had said. It did not look like a rock from outer space. It looked more like a piece from an airplane.

The object wasn't burning. The smoke came from a few cornstalks that had caught fire from the crash. The farmer bent down to get a closer look.

"Don't touch it!" cried Martha.

"Oh, for Pete's sake, Martha," he said. "I just want to —"

"What was that?" cried Martha.

Soon, a hissing sound filled the crater. A metal panel on top of the strange object began to open up. Martha and Jonathan both froze.

Two tiny hands rose up from the opening. A small head covered in dark hair peeked over the edge.

Martha ran down into the crater. "It's a baby!" she said.

"It's a little boy," said Jonathan, stunned.

A toddler looked up at them from the shiny object. A wide grin stretched across his happy face. He held out his arms, wanting to be picked up.

"Where did you come from, little man?" asked Jonathan.

"A baby!" repeated Martha.

"Yes, I can see that, Martha," he said.

"We always wanted to have a baby of our own," she said.

"He doesn't belong to us," Jonathan pointed out.

Martha reached out and lifted the toddler into her arms. "I don't think his family is from around here," she said. "Unless you see someone else falling from the sky."

"Oh, Martha," said her husband.

Martha Kent stared happily at the little boy. He smiled and grabbed at her hair. "I think we'll call you Clark," she said. "I've always liked that name."

Jonathan shook his head. "We can't do this, Martha," he said.

Martha stuck out her chin. "We're only going to take care of Clark until someone else comes looking for him," she said.

Martha looked up at the sky and then back at her husband. "But somehow I don't think that's going to happen. Do you?" she asked.

Jonathan put his arm around his wife's shoulders. The new family walked away from the crater and headed toward their house.

CHAPTER 5

SUPERPOWERS

Late that night, Jonathan and Martha hitched the strange object to the back of their combine. No one else saw them drag it into their barn. Then Jonathan began to dig a hole in the center of the barn's dirt floor.

"I don't want any nosy reporters looking for this thing," said Jonathan. "They'd never leave us alone."

Martha agreed. She was also worried that Clark might be taken away from them.

While Jonathan kept digging, Martha carefully searched the inside of the metal ship. She looked for clues about the strange baby. There were no photos, no toys, and no clothes.

"Look at this," Martha cried.

Her hand touched a bundle of red and blue blankets. She pulled them out and examined them closely.

"I wonder if these are from Clark's home," she said.

Once Jonathan buried the ship, they returned to the house. Martha walked upstairs and tucked the blankets deep inside a clothes chest in her bedroom.

"Clark may need these some day," she said to herself.

Over the next few days, Clark was a happy toddler. He enjoyed his new home. He was interested in the cows, the tractor, and the dogs. But most of the time, Clark stayed close by Martha. Something in her tender voice was comforting to him.

When Martha worked in the garden, Clark sat next to her. He dug his fists into the dirt. Martha would brush off a carrot or peapod and hand it to him. Then the boy would hungrily stuff it into his mouth.

That summer in Kansas was one of the hottest on record. Martha worked in the garden in the afternoons, when the sun was behind the big barn.

Clark didn't seem to mind the heat. The little boy didn't sweat. His skin didn't burn. In fact, Clark was happiest when sitting outside in the hot yellow rays of the sun.

ZHHINNGG!

Clark looked up at the weather vane on top of the house. It was spinning wildly. Martha noticed it too.

"Jonathan," she yelled. "I think we're in for a storm."

Jonathan was fixing some equipment in the barn. He didn't hear his wife's voice.

Martha stood up from the garden. She stretched her back. She was about to grab her buckets of carrots when she stopped.

Off to the southwest, the sky had grown greenish-black. Dangerous clouds drifted toward them. In the middle of the dark clouds, a gray cloud was spinning. It spun like the weather vane. Martha watched as a tongue of twisting air dropped from the sky.

As soon as the twister touched the ground, the tongue changed color. Now it was dark brown, the color of the dirt it was scooping up into its deadly funnel.

"Jonathan!" screamed Martha. "A twister! There's a twister!"

The whirling storm was heading toward the farm. Martha reached down and grabbed Clark's arm. She pulled him along behind her. They raced toward the storm shelter at the side of the house.

By the time they reached the shelter, powerful winds began to blow across the fields. The corn was pushed flat to the ground. The trees groaned and creaked. The weather vane suddenly snapped off the roof. It landed nearby on the ground, nearly hitting Martha and Clark.

Martha screamed again for her husband. She pulled open one of the storm shelter doors. It was low on the ground. Short wooden steps led down to a shelter built under the house.

"Jonathan!" she yelled again. "Where is your father?" Martha cried to Clark.

The little boy stared up at her face, puzzled. He could tell she was frightened. Things were falling around her, scaring her.

Clark was reminded of something that had happened far away. He didn't like it when people were afraid.

Finally, Martha saw Jonathan step out of the barn. "Here!" she yelled, waving her arms. "We're back here."

Jonathan ran toward her.

The sound of moaning metal grew louder than the storm.

Jonathan stopped and turned. He glanced at the silo that stood between the barn and the house.

The metal tower was rocking slowly back and forth. It began to pull away from its cement floor.

Another, louder, groan filled the air.

Jonathan was frozen with surprise as he watched the silo fall onto the ground.

Then he started running again. "Hurry! Hurry!" Martha yelled to him.

She turned to Clark, to push him into the storm shelter. The boy was gone.

Martha looked up at Jonathan. She wanted to yell at him, but the winds were too loud. He would not hear her saying that Clark was missing.

Then she saw him. Clark had wandered around the side of the house. He stood directly in the path of the rolling silo. In a moment, the metal tower would crush him.

Martha started to run after him. She knew she was too far away to reach him in time. There was nothing else she could do. Suddenly, the silo was on top of Clark.

The boy raised his little hands. His tiny fingers reached out and grabbed the metal. The silo stopped. The tower buckled in at the point where Clark was standing.

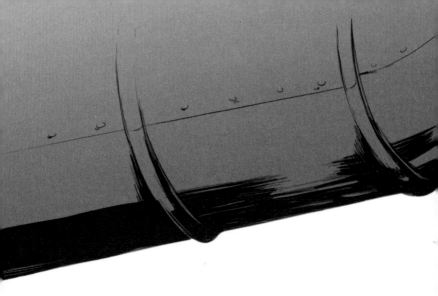

With a determined shove, Clark pushed
the silo away from him. It rolled harmlessly
across the cornfield.

Martha ran toward Clark and grabbed
him. Jonathan joined them. Then all three
hurried to the storm shelter and bolted the
door behind them.

While the winds screamed above them,
the family sat in the dim light of a small
lamp. Martha never let go of Clark.

His arms stayed wrapped around her neck. Jonathan gazed at his newly adopted son.

"You did see what happened, didn't you, Martha?" he asked quietly.

Martha nodded, tears in her eyes. "We rescued Clark, and now he rescued us," she replied.

Jonathan took off his glasses and wiped them with a rag. "He's just a baby now," he said. "Think of what he could do when he grows up."

"We'll be good parents," said Martha softly. "We'll raise him up as best we can."

Jonathan nodded. Then he reached over and patted the boy's shoulder. "You're a good boy, Clark," he said. "You did good, son."

The little hero looked up and smiled.

DAILY PLANET

FROM THE DESK OF CLARK KENT

WHO IS SUPERMAN?

As young Kal-El grew, he quickly discovered that his extraordinary abilities didn't end with superstrength. The yellow sun of Earth fueled his muscles with a variety of superpowers, including X-ray vision, bulletproof skin, and the ability to fly. Instead of using his powers against others, Kal-El chose to become Earth's guardian. He became Superman, the Last Son of Krypton. As the world's greatest super hero, he defends the planet against danger and the forces of evil.

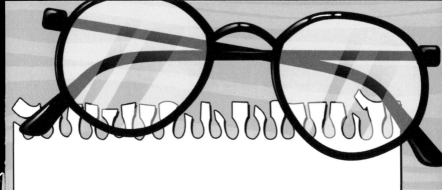

- Martha Kent created the iconic blue and red costume for her adopted son. The invisible, solar-charged aura around Superman's skin protects the suit from damage.

- Although blessed with great powers, Superman also has some weaknesses. The Man of Steel cannot defend himself against magic. He is also powerless against kryptonite, a radioactive material from his home planet Krypton.

- The Man of Steel must protect his super hero identity. He spends most of his day as Clark Kent, a mild-mannered reporter for the Metropolis newspaper the Daily Planet.

- Every super hero needs a hideaway. Superman's secret base, the Fortress of Solitude, is located where no one will find it: the Arctic Circle.

BIOGRAPHIES

Michael Dahl is the author of more than 200 books for children and young adults. He has won the AEP Distinguished Achievement Award three times for his non-fiction. His Finnegan Zwake mystery series was shortlisted twice by the Anthony and Agatha awards. He has also written the *Library of Doom* series and the *Dragonblood* books. He is a featured speaker at conferences around the country on graphic novels and high-interest books for boys.

John Delaney is an award-winning storyboard artist, director, animator and design artist with over 20 years of experience in both live-action production and animation. For the past 15 years John has also worked as a comic book artist for DC Comics and Bongo Comics. He has pencilled a wide variety of characters such as Superman, Batman, Wonder Woman and the Justice League, as well as shows like *Dexter's Laboratory*, *Scooby-Doo*, *Futurama*, *The Simpsons*, and many more.

Lee Loughridge has been working in comics for over 14 years. He currently resides in sunny California in a tent on the beach.

GLOSSARY

chamber (CHAYM-bur)—a large room

cocoon (kuh-KOON)—a protective covering

combine (KOM-bahyn)—a harvesting machine used for cutting grain in the field

cooing (KOO-ing)—making sweet and soft sounds

council (KOUN-sil)—a group of people chosen to watch over a city

phase (FAZE)—a temporary stage in a cycle

shattered (SHAT-urd)—broke into tiny pieces

supercomputer (soo-per-kom-PYOO-tur)—a very fast, powerful computer that is used for complex calculations

troopers (TROO-pur)—a soldier in an army

weather vane (WETH-er VEYN)—a device that uses a rod and a rotating pointer to indicate the direction of the wind

DISCUSSION QUESTIONS

1. Why do you think the Kents decided to keep their discovery a secret? Do you think some secrets are okay? Explain your answer.

2. In the story, Brainiac escapes the planet Krypton before it explodes. What do you think will happen to him? Will Superman and Brainiac ever meet?

3. At the end of the story, the Kents know that Kal-El will grow up to do great things. Discuss some things you know about Superman that weren't described in the story. What are his other superpowers? Who are some of his enemies?

WRITING PROMPTS

1. This book only tells the story of Superman as a child. Write your own story about Superman as a teenager or an adult.

2. Describe your own origin story. Where were you born? What were your first words? If you don't know, ask a parent or guardian for help. Once you've collected the information, write a story about it.

3. Many books are written and illustrated by two different people. Write a story, and then give it to a friend to illustrate the pictures.

MORE NEW SUPERMAN ADVENTURES!

THE MENACE OF METALLO

THE MUSEUM MONSTERS

THE STOLEN SUPERPOWERS

TOYS OF TERROR

UNDER THE RED SUN